Welcome to ALADDIN QUIX!

If you are looking for fast, fun-to-read stories with colorful characters, lots of kid-friendly humor, easy-to-follow action, entertaining story lines, and lively illustrations, then **ALADDIN QUIX** is for you!

But wait, there's more!

If you're also looking for stories with tables of contents; word lists; about-the-book questions; 64, 80, or 96 pages; short chapters; short paragraphs; and large fonts, then **ALADDIN QUIX** is *definitely* for you!

ALADDIN QUIX: The next step between ready to reads and longer, more challenging chapter books, for readers five to eight years old.

Read more ALADDIN QUIX books!

By Stephanie Calmenson

Our Principal Is a Frog!
Our Principal Is a Wolf!
Our Principal's in His Underwear!
Our Principal Breaks a Spell!

A Miss Mallard Mystery
By Robert Quackenbush

Dig to Disaster
Texas Trail to Calamity
Express Train to Trouble
Stairway to Doom

Little Goddess Girls
By Joan Holub and Suzanne Williams

Book 1: *Athena & the Magic Land*
Book 2: *Persephone & the Giant Flowers*
Book 3: *Aphrodite & the Gold Apple*

Mack Rhino, Private Eye
By Jennifer Swender and Paul DuBois Jacobs

Book 1: *The Big Race Lace Case*
Book 2: *The Candy Caper Case*

Fort Builders
By Dee Romito

Book 1: *The Birthday Castle*
Book 2: *Happy Tails Lodge*
Book 3: *Battle of the Blanket Forts*

ELF ACADEMY

TROUBLE IN TOYLAND

BY **ALAN KATZ**

ILLUSTRATED BY
SERNUR IŞIK

Ⓠ QUIX

ALADDIN QUIX

NEW YORK   LONDON   TORONTO   SYDNEY   NEW DELHI

To my wonderful, creative friend Jaida Blatt

—A. K.

ALADDIN QUIX

Simon & Schuster Children's Publishing Division

1230 Avenue of the Americas, New York, New York 10020

First Aladdin QUIX hardcover edition September 2021

Text copyright © 2021 by Simon & Schuster, Inc.

Illustrations copyright © 2021 by Sernur Işik

Also available in an Aladdin QUIX paperback edition.

All rights reserved, including the right of reproduction in whole or in part in any form.

ALADDIN and the related marks and colophon are trademarks of Simon & Schuster, Inc.

For information about special discounts for bulk purchases, please contact Simon & Schuster Special Sales at 1-866-506-1949 or business@simonandschuster.com.

The Simon & Schuster Speakers Bureau can bring authors to your live event. For more information or to book an event contact the Simon & Schuster Speakers Bureau at 1-866-248-3049 or visit our website at www.simonspeakers.com.

Designed by Tiara Iandiorio

The illustrations for this book were rendered digitally.

The text of this book was set in Archer Medium.

Manufactured in the United States of America 0821 LAK

2 4 6 8 10 9 7 5 3 1

Library of Congress Control Number 2021940158

ISBN 978-1-5344-6789-7 (hc)

ISBN 978-1-5344-6788-0 (pbk)

ISBN 978-1-5344-6790-3 (ebook)

Cast of Characters

Andy Snowden: An Elf Academy student

Ms. Dow: The second-grade teacher at Elf Academy

Jay: Andy's best friend

Principal Evergreen: The principal at Elf Academy

Craig Snowden: Andy's older brother

Santa Claus: Jolly gift giver

Susu Snowden: Andy's twin sister

Nicole: Susu's best friend

Mr. and Ms. Snowden: Parents of Andy, Susu, and Craig

Kal: An Elf Academy student

Zahara: An Elf Academy student

Jenny: An Elf Academy student

Mrs. Claus: The first lady of the North Pole

Contents

1

Helmet High Jinks

The toy-building **workshop** at Elf Academy is a happy, busy place.

Look around, and you'll see wheels for trucks, game pieces, guitar strings, bouncy springs, and buttons of all sizes. Those parts will help create exciting toys, thanks to . . .

Dozens of smiling, hard-working elves.

Every morning, **Andy Snowden** and his second-grade classmates study math, science, reading, and history. And every after-noon, they snap, paste, and ham-mer during toy-building lessons. Everyone loves those lessons the most.

Well, *almost everyone*, that is.

Andy certainly enjoys building toys.

But he is not happy making the same exact ones, day after day after day. Andy is tired of putting together hundreds of:

- yo-yos
- airplanes
- chess sets
- rubber ducks
- royal castles
- teeny-tiny frogs
- lime-green pianos
- rainbow bubble blowers

- shiny superhero capes
- walkie-talkies

Not to mention . . . lots and lots of creepy-crawly caterpillars.

So this coming holiday season, Andy is itching to build something different. He really wants to use his **imagination**.

☆ ☆ ☆

"Watch this, everybody! Twenty-two, twenty-three, twenty-

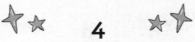

four . . . ," Andy said one day as he plopped a stack of outer-space helmets onto his head.

"Andy!" **Ms. Dow**, his teacher, called out. "Please take off each and every one of those helmets. Right now!"

"I know, I know, Ms. Dow. They are gifts that we built for

children around the world," Andy said. "I'm sorry, but I wanted to set a record for wearing the *most* helmets. I thought a good laugh would help the other elves make happier toys."

As Andy removed the giant pile from his head, his best friend, **Jay**, whispered to him, "I bet you could have reached fifty!"

"Thanks, Jay," Andy answered as he carefully placed the helmets into gift boxes.

"Now, Andy, laughter is a good

thing," Ms. Dow said. "But this is work time," she told him.

"Most of all," she continued, "you must remember the Elf Academy rules: We do not play with the toys we build. We do not wear the helmets we **construct**.

"And what else, class . . . ?"

"We do not ride the tricycles, bicycles, and especially unicycles that we've put together!" everyone said.

(That rule had been added after

Andy had taken a speedy ride

across the workshop a few weeks

before.)

Crrrrrash!

After Andy put the helmets away, Ms. Dow spoke to the class. "I know that you've all been working hard for months. But it's almost Christmas, and we will be busier than ever these last few weeks."

The elves nodded.

Ms. Dow continued, "**Principal Evergreen** would like all the second graders to meet at the Snowflake Auditorium this afternoon. She has an important **announcement**."

Andy and his classmates were a little nervous. Christmas was near. What could be more important than spending time making toys?

2

Bird Contest

All the second graders filed into the hall. Paintings of snowy mountains and chimney tops, as well as Elf Academy class pictures, lined the walls.

On the way to the auditorium,

Andy glanced at one of his favorite photographs: his older brother **Craig**'s fourth-grade class picture. In it, all the elves were stacked like a **pyramid**, waving and smiling, and their teacher stood nearby. Andy knew that pose had been his brother's idea. Craig *always* had the best ideas.

When the elves were seated, Principal Evergreen walked out onto the stage. She had purple-and-orange **braided** hair that was piled high upon her head.

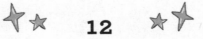

"Good afternoon, second grad-ers!" Principal Evergreen said with a big smile.

"Good afternoon, Principal Evergreen!" they answered. They held their breath, not sure what their principal would say next.

"First let me tell you about some of our new classes next term. You will all be studying world geog-raphy, the many sides of snow-flakes, **ancient** art history, and undersea creatures."

Andy and Jay gave each other

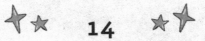

a thumbs-up. Ocean animals were some of Andy's favorites. He imagined that with eight arms an octopus would be super helpful at making toys.

Then their principal continued. "Now I have some exciting news."

Everyone's ears **tingled**.

"For the first time ever, we are holding an Elf Academy Toy-Building Contest. Each of the second graders will design and build a bird of their choice.

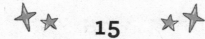

The students will select one of the birds as the Toy of the Year."

"YAHOO!" Andy cheered. Everyone turned to look at him.

"Shhhh, Andy," Jay whispered. "You'll get in trouble."

Principal Evergreen smiled. "'Yahoo' is right, Andy."

Then she continued speaking to all the elves. "Once a toy wins the vote, you will then make many more, and **Santa Claus** will bring them to children around the world. Your teachers will give you the instruc-

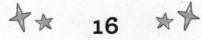

tions for the contest when you get back to class. **Good luck!**"

Once back in class, Ms. Dow shared the contest rules:

- Second-grade elves will be asked to make a bird.
- You can choose whatever kind of bird you wish.
- You can use whatever materials are in the workshop.
- You will have one hour to complete your project.
- **Have fun!**

"We will get started first thing tomorrow afternoon," she told the elves. "I hope you are as excited as I am!"

3

Lots of Decisions

After school Andy, his twin sister, **Susu**, and Susu's best friend, **Nicole**, walked home together.

"I love hummingbirds," Susu said. "That's what I'm going to make."

"And I'm going to make a pea-cock," Nicole told her friends. "I know it won't be easy because they have such fancy tails, but I'll try."

Andy had no idea what kind of bird he would try to build. There

were so many different kinds in
the world. How could he choose?
He knew that toucans had colorful beaks. Flamingos could bal-
ance on one foot. And ostriches
had eyes bigger than any other
land animal.

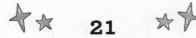

Andy was sure that he could make a great space helmet, skateboard, or dollhouse, but he had never created a bird before. Maybe Craig could help him later when they were home.

☆ ☆ ☆

The Snowdens' blue-and-green house was smack in the middle of North Pole Avenue.

It was **surrounded** by yellow-and-purple, pink-and-orange, and

black-and-white houses—some tall, some short, some round, some square, some shaped like tri-angles.

Mr. and Ms. Snowden had to take Susu to a Snow Scouts meeting, so that gave Andy and Craig time to talk about the Elf Academy contest.

"I've never created a bird," Andy said. "I was excited when Principal Evergreen announced the contest, but I'm not really sure what to do."

Craig picked up four balls and started juggling. "A good bird needs interesting parts. Like baseballs. Or maybe wagon wheels. Kite tails. Perhaps water balloons."

Andy giggled. "Craig! **Stop joking!**" he said.

Craig's ideas might have been silly, but they did make Andy think.

Getting creative, he said to himself. *Is that what it takes to make a great bird?*

4

Time to Build

Andy had a very hard time waking up the next morning. All night long he had tossed and turned and turned and tossed, with **visions** of different types of birds running through his mind.

By the time he got dressed and rushed downstairs, Craig and Susu had already finished their snowberries-and-oatmeal smoothies and were halfway out the door.

"Wait for me!" Andy called. He gulped down his smoothie, slipped into his jacket, and ran after his brother and sister.

Andy was usually a laughing, joking chatterbox when he, Susu, and Craig walked to school.

But today he was silent.

And he was worried.

Susu looked over at her twin brother. "Is everything okay, Andy? You haven't cracked one corny joke."

"Well, well . . . ," Andy began.

"Well what?" Craig asked.

"I still can't decide what type of bird to make for the contest," Andy told them.

As they reached the Elf Academy entrance, Craig smiled at him and said, "Don't worry. You'll find a way to be creative. You *always* do."

Andy wasn't so sure about that.

Morning classes passed quickly— too quickly for Andy. Usually he couldn't wait to make toys, but today he was last in line when the elves marched to the workshop.

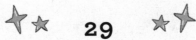

Large tables were covered with different-colored feathers and **sturdy** wings, plus beaks, eyes, legs, and feet. The elves gasped with excitement.

Ms. Dow said, "Class, feel free to use all of these materials. You will have one hour to complete your project. And as Principal Evergreen said, have fun!"

More than anything else, Andy wanted to have fun. But if he wasn't sure about the kind of bird he was going to make for the

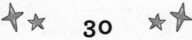

contest, how *could* he have fun?

He raised his hand to ask a question.

"Yes, Andy?" Ms. Dow asked.

"Can we build as many birds as we want?" Andy wanted to know.

"I'm sorry, Andy," Ms. Dow replied. "Each elf is allowed to make *one* bird, and one bird only. So do your best."

Andy nodded.

He looked around the work-shop at:

- the different shapes and shades of feathers,
- realistic, **birdlike** feathers,
- the pointy beaks and the rounded ones,
- the feet that were webbed and ones that were clawed ...

And then ...

He *finally* had an idea!

5

Imagine That

"When I ring this bell, the bird making may begin," Ms. Dow **informed** the elves. *DING!*

The elves rushed toward the supply tables. In no time at all, feathers were flying!

"I want the blue beak," called **Kal**.

Zahara said, "Pass me those sparkly eyes, please!"

"Is there another pair of webbed feet?" asked **Jenny**.

Everyone made their choices and then walked quickly to their tables.

Everyone but Andy, who gathered up all the extra supplies.

Andy stared at the huge pile in front of him, but he still didn't know where to begin. He tried putting a feather here and placing a beak there.

He looked over at the other elves, who were busily building.

Susu was gluing feet onto the tiny purple hummingbird she was creating.

Nicole was placing just the right dark blue feathers for her **majestic** peacock.

Jay was making a cardinal, using most of the red paint in the workshop to make it look real.

Andy carefully studied each piece and part.

And just like an eight-armed octopus, he started building!

A little glue here.

A twist-snap-twist there.

Then he added a beak, feathers, and claws.

Andy was so busy that he didn't bother checking the clock.

 38

But then he heard Ms. Dow say, "Six minutes left, class. **Start finishing up!**"

Finish up? Andy said to himself. *But I'm just getting started!*

☆ ☆ ☆

DING! DING!

"Time's up, everyone," Ms. Dow announced. "Please stop building."

The elves all stood back to **reveal** their creations. Workbench

after workbench was filled with birds from redheaded wood-peckers to snowy owls to gold-finches.

"Good work, one and all," Ms. Dow said proudly. "Tomorrow morning we will find out which of you wins the contest. There is no homework tonight, so have a great evening."

As the elves started filing out of the classroom, Susu passed her brother's workbench.

She stopped. She looked at his

40

toy design. And she blurted out, "Andy! **What in the North Pole did you build?**"

Andy had been feeling happy about what he had made. But now Susu made him sad. He threw a

cover over his toy and ran out of the room, with everyone laughing.

☆ ☆ ☆

During a game of Chimneys and Ladders later that day, Craig asked his brother and sister how the bird building had gone.

"Great!" Susu said. "I made a teeny-tiny hummingbird!"

Andy didn't respond. Instead he stopped playing the game and **slumped** in his chair.

"Andy, I'm sure you made something elf-tacular," Craig said to his brother. "Remember your super-sprinkle cookies? Or your windup flying robot? Every time we create something, we win, even if *you* don't win tomorrow."

"I guess," Andy said sadly.

Ms. Dow had wished the elves a great evening. But Andy's wasn't great at all. He even went to bed one hour before his normal bedtime.

Just like he had done the

night before, Andy tossed and turned and turned and tossed, worried he had made an elf-tastic mistake.

6

The Big Decision

The halls of Elf Academy were filled with **merriness** the next day. Teachers, students, and toy makers of every age couldn't wait to see what the second graders had made for the contest.

Andy asked himself, *What if everyone reacts the way Susu did? Did I overdo it?*

☆ ☆ ☆

The Snowflake Auditorium was buzzing with excitement; every seat was filled. A smiling Principal Evergreen strolled onto the stage. **"Good morning, elves!"** she said. "We are here to decide the winner of the first Elf Academy

Toy-Building Contest. Remember, second graders, there can be only one winner—but you are each a winner every time you create something."

Craig waved to his brother and mouthed, "That's what I told you!"

One by one the elves walked out onstage and showed off their feathered toys. As they did, the Gift-O-Meter recorded the audience's **applause**.

Nicole shared her jewel-colored peacock. Everyone clapped.

They also clapped when Susu held up her itty-bitty hummingbird.

Kal got cheers for his falcon,

which looked as if it were soaring high in the sky.

After everyone else had presented their contest entries, it was finally Andy's turn.

He walked to the center of the stage and slowly uncovered his toy. He was nervous, but he knew there was no turning back.

"Okay, everyone," he announced. "Get ready to meet the world's first . . . **GLOP CLOP PLOP!**"

"What . . . is . . . that?"

Ms. Dow asked. She couldn't believe her eyes. Neither could anyone else. Everyone started laughing and pointing.

Andy's face turned beet red. But he repeated, **"A GLOP CLOP PLOP."**

"Andy, there is no such thing," Ms. Dow insisted. "It doesn't look like any bird I've ever seen."

Everyone kept laughing. Andy wanted to run backstage, but when he looked out into the crowd, he spotted Craig. His brother smiled

at him and gave him a thumbs-up.

That was all Andy needed to continue.

He took a deep breath and said, "Ms. Dow, take a closer look. It looks like *many* birds you've seen from all around the world."

Andy began:

"*G* is for 'goose.'

L is for 'loon.'

O is for 'ostrich,' and

P is for 'parrot.'"

Andy pressed a button, and the bird said, "Pretty bird, pretty bird."

Then he continued,

"*C* is for 'cuckoo.'

L is for 'lark.'

O is for 'oriole,' and

P is for 'pelican.'"

Andy held up the toy, and a cuckoo sprung out of the bird's

mouth two times, to let everyone know that it was eleven o'clock. He continued:

"*P* is for 'penguin.'

L is for 'lovebird.'

O is for 'owl,' and

P is for 'puffin.'"

Andy grinned. "Do you see what I mean, Ms. Dow? *G-L-O-P C-L-O-P P-L-O-P!* One bird, so many ways to play."

No one said a word. It was so quiet, you could hear a snowflake drop.

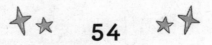

7

GLOP CLOP

Then suddenly Susu called out, "That's elf-tacular, Andy!"

"Way to go, Snowden!" cried Zahara.

One by one the elves stood up and gave Andy a standing **ovation**!

Their cheering and clapping, hooting and hollering shook the Snowflake Auditorium. Principal Evergreen started to ask everyone to quiet down. But it was such a happy moment that even she joined in the ovation.

Ms. Dow couldn't believe her ears. Or her eyes. She told Andy, "That's quite something. Wait until Santa and **Mrs. Claus** see—"

"Wait until Santa and Mrs. Claus see *what*?" a booming voice asked.

It was Santa! And Mrs. Claus! What a surprise. They walked down the center aisle of the auditorium, the elves cheering all over again.

"Yay! Hooray! It's a merry day!"

"Hello, Mr. and Mrs. Claus," Ms. Dow said, welcoming them to the Snowflake stage. "I was saying, 'Wait until Santa and Mrs. Claus see how creative a second-grade elf can be.'"

Andy carefully handed the Clauses his toy, and they closely **inspected** every inch of Andy's work. The elf explained why it was called a **GLOP CLOP PLOP**.

Mrs. Claus's eyes twinkled.

"Why, Andy, it's twelve toys in one!" she exclaimed.

"Santa, isn't this just like the **SHEP SHOP** you made when you were a little boy?" she asked.

"A SHEP SHOP? What is that?" Ms. Dow asked.

Andy's ears tingled, his nose twitched, and his eyes sparkled. Before Santa could reply, Andy took a guess. "Was your toy a

Swan

Hawk

Emu

Partridge

Sparrow

Heron

Osprey

Parakeet?" he asked.

Santa beamed. "That's it on the nose, Andy. And it was *always* my favorite toy."

Santa turned to Ms. Dow and asked, "May Mrs. Claus and I have the honor of checking the Gift-O-Meter to see which toy is the contest winner?"

"Certainly," Ms. Dow said.

Principal Evergreen nodded as well, and the Clauses **examined** the machine. A few moments later they walked to center stage, gazing out at the crowd.

"Second graders," Santa began, "you all received very high scores, but we can plainly see the winner is . . ."

"Andy Snowden and his **GLOP CLOP PLOP**!" Mrs. Claus announced.

The elves shrieked so loudly that the hands on the Gift-O-Meter started spinning out of control.

Santa continued, "Elf Academy elves, please start building Andy's birds for children everywhere. **Ho ho ho!** And goodbye, all!" With that, he and Mrs. Claus left the auditorium.

Ms. Dow smiled and said, "Okay, elves, you heard Santa. Let's get busy."

"One moment, Ms. Dow," Principal Evergreen interrupted. "Before the second graders start working, the entire academy is

invited to celebrate in the lunchroom with doughnuts and hot
cocoa."

Walking through the halls to
the lunchroom, kindergartners
through fifth graders congratu-
lated Andy, shaking his hand,

patting his back. He still couldn't believe his still-tingling ears.

Susu couldn't either. "Toys for kids all over the world? That's amazing!"

Jay was grinning too. "We've never had doughnuts before lunch. **Yum!**"

Andy couldn't wait to get to the workshop and start building. He had followed directions and made just *one* bird, but it was a bird that had let him fully use his imagination. Soon kids all over

the world would have a **GLOP CLOP PLOP** of their own.

But Andy knew exactly who he was going to give the very first—or really the *second*—one to: Craig, who had believed in Andy and his imagination, from the start.

Word List

ancient (AINT•shent): Something that has been around for a very long time

announcement (uh•NOUNT•smunt): A public statement

applause (uh•PLOZ): Approval shown by clapping hands

birdlike (BURD•lyke): Looking like some part of an animal with two wings, two feet, and a body covered with feathers

braided (BRAY•did): Having

three or more woven strands

construct (con•STRUKT): To build or make something

dozens (DUH•zins): Groups of twelve

examined (ig•ZA•mund): Looked at carefully

imagination (ih•ma•juh•NAY•shun): Creative ability

informed (in•FORMD): Gave information to someone

inspected (in•SPEK•ted): Looked at closely

majestic (muh•JEH•stik):

Having or showing greatness

merriness (MER•ee•ness):
A feeling of gladness and
excitement

ovation (oh•VAY•shun): Excited
standing and clapping

pyramid (PIHR•uh•mid): A
shape that is wide at the bottom
and narrows gradually as it
reaches the top

reveal (ree•VEEL): To show
something that was hidden before

slumped (SLUMPT): Dropped
down

sturdy (STUR•dee): Firmly built or made

surrounded (suh•ROUN•ded): Closed in on all sides

tingled (TIN•guld): Had a prickling or thrilling feeling

visions (VIH•zhuns): Things imagined or seen in dreams

workshop (WURK•shop): A place where things are made or built

Questions

1. How many helmets did Andy have on this head when Ms. Dow asked him to take them off?

2. Which one-wheeled item were the elves told not to ride?

3. If you could make a bird or any other creature like the GLOP CLOP PLOP, what would it be?

4. Why couldn't Andy fall asleep the first night? Why couldn't

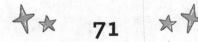

he fall asleep the second
night?

5. What did Andy's brother, Craig,
tell Andy to help him feel
better?